If the Shoe Fits

Gary Soto

illustrated by
Terry Widener

G. P. Putnam's Sons

Rigo had three brothers and one sister, and when you counted his parents and Uncle Celso, who lived with them, his home was as crowded as a bus.

He didn't really mind the noisy house. What Rigo minded most were his hand-me-down clothes.

His oldest brother, Hector, passed his shirts and pants down to Manuel, who passed them to Carlos, who passed them to Rigo.

Rigo passed them into the garbage can.

"Mom, I need some new clothes!" Rigo cried
one day when he put on a jacket that Carlos had
outgrown.

Two buttons were missing and the fabric was faded.

"*Mi'jo*, new clothes cost money," his mother said.

When Rigo started to pout, Uncle Celso brought
out his old wallet and handed Rigo a five-dollar bill.

"Let me help you," Uncle said.

Rigo refused the money. He didn't want to tell his
uncle that new clothes cost more than that.

But for Rigo's ninth birthday, his mom bought him a pair of brand-new shoes. They were called loafers. They were the fanciest shoes Rigo had ever owned. They didn't even have laces to drag in the dirt.

"Put a penny in them," Rigo's sister, Theresa, said. "That's the style."

But instead of worthless pennies, Rigo pushed in nickels.

"There," he said. He slipped into his new shoes and clicked his heels together.

That day Rigo marched down the street, grinning proudly at his shoes. He liked how the nickels glinted in the sunlight.

At the corner playground some kids were throwing water balloons at each other. Rigo wanted to join them but was afraid he might ruin his shoes.

Suddenly Angel sneaked up from behind and yelled, "Hey, how come you got nickels in your shoes? You ain't rich!"

"It's the style," Rigo answered.

"There ain't no style like that!" Angel growled. "Nobody wears those kind of stupid shoes!"

Then Angel demanded the nickels from Rigo's shoes.

"Nah, Angel!" Rigo begged. "I don't want to mess up my new loafers. It was hard to put the nickels in."

"Forget your loafers!" Angel snapped. And he ripped the nickels from the slots.

Rigo went home and threw his shoes into the closet.

But at the end of the summer he changed his mind. He had received an invitation to a birthday party. It was from Kristie Hernandez. No girl had ever invited him to a birthday party before.

On the day of the party, Rigo brushed his teeth extra hard and combed his hair four different ways. He settled on slicking his hair back. He felt *suave*. Next he put on his newest-looking hand-me-downs, and finally he got his fancy loafers from the closet.

"Come on," he grunted, trying to cram his feet into the shoes.

When he stood up, he knew the shoes were too tight. Pain stabbed the top of his feet as he took a step. He took off the torture shoes and stretched them, yanking on the leather. He put on his thinnest socks, even though they had holes in the heels.

Rigo left the house walking stiffly. After three painful blocks, he wished he were crawling instead of walking. But lucky for him, he discovered that his feet didn't hurt so much if he walked backwards. He walked like that all the way to the party.

"Nice shoes," Kristie said, greeting him at the door.

"Thanks," said Rigo, trying to smile. He didn't want to tell her that they were killing his feet. He was sure that he had blood blisters and one of his little toes had fallen off. "But if you don't mind, I'm going to take them off."

"Why?" Kristie asked.

Rigo's mind whirled for an answer.

He clicked his fingers and said, "To play soccer!"

When he scored two goals, his feet felt better.

Over dinner that night, Rigo told his family that Kristie's party was great. "Everyone was there! José-Luis, Julie, Debbie, Joey, Carolina, Lupe, Rachel, Sofia, Martin, Jaime, Lily, Maya, and Maya's little sister, I forgot her name, plus some little cousins of Kristie's who were still in their diapers . . ."

"*¡Híjole!* That's a lot of kids to feed!" Uncle Celso remarked.

"Yeah, but a party's more fun with lots of kids," Rigo said.

"Next year, *mi'jo*, we can have a party for you like that," his uncle said. "And you know why?"

Rigo shook his head.

"Because I have a new job as a waiter!" Uncle announced. "I'll make a lot of money— *¡mucho dinero!*"

After dinner, Uncle Celso began to gather the dirty plates from the table. Rigo's father protested, "Leave them for the kids."

"No, *hombre*, I have to practice being a waiter," Uncle said.

"I'll help with the dishes," said Rigo. He liked to be with Uncle and listen to his stories about Mexico.

Rigo rolled up the sleeves of his sweatshirt.

As the two worked side by side, Rigo noticed that he was slightly taller than Uncle.

He noticed that Uncle's pants were too loose for him and that his shirt had flecks of paint on it. He looked at Uncle's shoes.

The next morning Rigo brought his loafers to
the couch, where Uncle slept.

"*¿Qué es esto?*" Uncle asked, opening one eye.
"What's this?"

"A present for you. Kind of used, but try them on!"

Uncle sat up and took the shoes.

"These are the most beautiful shoes I've ever had," he said. He patted Rigo's cheek.

"You don't mind if they're hand-me-downs?" Rigo asked.

"Hand-me-downs, nothing!" Uncle said.
"These are brand-new! I can go to work in style!"
He tapped on the soles and then put them on. He
squinted an eye at his nephew. "Are you sure you
want to give them to me?"

"Yeah, I'm sure," Rigo said. "To tell you the
truth, Uncle, I like them, but they hurt my feet.
I grew a little."

Uncle reached for his front pocket.

"These coins are older than I am," Uncle said. He held up two *centavos*, brown as his own skin, and smiled. "They're kind of like hand-me-downs too."

When Rigo took the old Mexican coins, he knew what to do with them—fit them into the slots of his new loafers, if he ever got any. Next time around he would wear them no matter what people like Angel said.

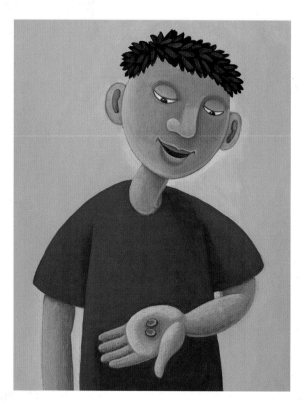

To Gabriella and Jamie,
barefoot and running . . . —G. S.

To C. S. M.,
hope your new shoe is a fit. —T. W.

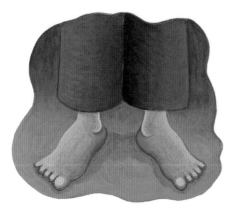

GLOSSARY:

centavos   Mexican pennies

¡Híjole!   Wow!

hombre   man

mi'jo   my son

mucho dinero   a lot of money

¿Qué es esto?   What is this?

suave   sophisticated

Library of Congress Cataloging-in-Publication Data   Soto, Gary. If the shoe fits / by Gary Soto; illustrated by Terry Widener.   p.   cm. Summary: After being teased about his brand-new loafers, Rigo puts them away for so long he grows out of them. [1. Shoes—Fiction. 2. Uncles—Fiction. 3. Teasing—Fiction. 4. Mexican Americans—Fiction.] I. Widener, Terry, ill. II. Title. PZ7.S7242 If 2002 [E]—dc21 00-068413 ISBN 0-399-23420-9 10 9 8 7 6 5 4 3 2 1
First Impression